PUBLIC LIBR

P9-DEV-420
FISHERS

This Book Belongs To:

j PIC BK Ran
Ransome, James.
 My teacher
2011023709
9780803732599

INV 10/12

10/18

My Teacher

by James Ransome

Dial Books for Young Readers
an imprint of Penguin Group (USA) Inc.

Kangaroo

Chee

DIAL BOOKS FOR YOUNG READERS
A division of Penguin Young Readers Group • Published by The Penguin
Group • Penguin Group (USA) Inc., 375 Hudson Street, New York, NY 10014,
U.S.A. • Penguin Group (Canada), 90 Eglinton Avenue East, Suite 700,
Toronto, • Ontario, Canada M4P 2Y3 (a division of Pearson Penguin Canada
Inc.) • Penguin Books Ltd, 80 Strand, London WC2R 0RL, England • Penguin
Ireland, 25 St. Stephen's Green, Dublin 2, Ireland (a division of Penguin
Books Ltd) • Penguin Group (Australia), 250 Camberwell Road, Camberwell,
Victoria 3124, Australia (a division of Pearson Australia Group Pty Ltd) •
Penguin Books India Pvt Ltd, 11 Community Centre, Panchsheel Park, New
Delhi - 110 017, India • Penguin Group (NZ), 67 Apollo Drive, Rosedale,
Auckland 0632, New Zealand (a division of Pearson New Zealand Ltd) •
Penguin Books (South Africa) (Pty) Ltd, 24 Sturdee Avenue, Rosebank,
Johannesburg 2196, South Africa • Penguin Books Ltd, Registered Offices:
80 Strand, London WC2R 0RL, England

Copyright © 2012 by James Ransome • All rights reserved
The publisher does not have any control over and does not assume any
responsibility for author or third-party websites or their content.

Designed by Mina Chung • Text set in Gotham Rounded
Manufactured in China on acid-free paper
10 9 8 7 6 5 4 3 2 1

Library of Congress Cataloging-in-Publication Data
Ransome, James.
My teacher / by James Ransome.
              p. cm.
Summary: A student wonders why her teacher has chosen to teach in
her school for so long, and highlights all the special things her teacher
does for her class.
ISBN 978-0-8037-3259-9 (hardcover)
[1. Teachers—Fiction. 2. Schools—Fiction.] I. Title.
PZ7.R1755My 2011 [E]—dc23
              2011023709

To all the dedicated teachers who come in early, leave late, and give a little something extra for the students.

A special thanks to my high school teacher, Charlie Bogasat, for all the extras.

— J.R.

My teacher has been teaching at my school for a long time. Some people joke and say she was teaching before schools were even built.

I know that's not true, but she did teach my mama and my grandmama.

Some people wonder why my teacher teaches in my school.

She could have retired a long time ago.

She could teach across town, where the sun always shines.

Maybe I know why she keeps teaching here.

My teacher calls us her Writing Bees, because every morning we are busy with our journal writing. I love writing stories, especially about princesses who slay dragons to save the prince.

My teacher says that I'm a good storyteller and that I should think about being an author when I grow up. My teacher loves for us to use our talents. Maybe that's why she keeps teaching.

We don't have a library in our school, but one day my teacher came to school with boxes and boxes of books. "We are making our own classroom library," said my teacher. "Fiction on this side and nonfiction on that side."

My teacher loves to read and she makes us love
it too. Maybe that's why she keeps teaching.

The next day my teacher was reading us a story about fathers when my friend Erin started crying. She said that her parents are getting a divorce. My teacher closed the book right away, and we began discussing different types of families. Later she took out crayons and paper and asked us to draw family portraits.

After we came back from lunch everyone had to stand next to their drawing and tell us who was in their family. One boy had two uncles, an aunt, and five cousins living in his apartment.

My teacher likes to talk about things that are important to us. Maybe that's why she keeps teaching.

One day my teacher read us a story about a jazz musician named Duke Ellington, which we all loved. Then she brought out her jazz records and old record player. She taught us that there are different styles of jazz. She likes big band jazz the best because you can dance to it.

"In Harlem there was a dance hall called the Savoy Ballroom and they did a swing dance called the Lindy hop," said my teacher.

I asked her if she could show us the Lindy hop. And we spent the day listening to jazz and dancing and dancing and dancing.

Now when I'm at home listening to music on the radio I can sometimes hear a little jazz in my favorite songs and that makes me smile.

A few weeks before Thanksgiving my teacher came to school with lots of empty cardboard boxes and a big bag of green pencils with white flowers. Everyone in our school donates food so we can fill up the boxes for people in our neighborhood. When I asked my teacher why, she said, "We don't always know what challenges others have at home." She says, "It is always important to help others in need."

The boxes were all filled with food a week before Thanksgiving. When I was putting on my coat to go home that day, I noticed my teacher placing the flower pencils in each box. I wished that I could have one of those pencils too.

Then yesterday, when I asked Nola if I could borrow a pencil, she handed me one of the pencils my teacher had placed in those boxes. I'm glad we could help Nola's family with our donation.

A couple of weeks ago my teacher said, "You are going to begin your first big project. You'll write a report and draw a picture of someone from the nonfiction section of our class library." We could choose anyone we liked: a famous artist, an author, inventor, astronaut, or a president of the United States.

I picked Langston Hughes. He was a great poet during the Harlem Renaissance. We did some research on the computer and used books from the public library. I was very surprised to find out that many of the poems Langston Hughes wrote were based on jazz.

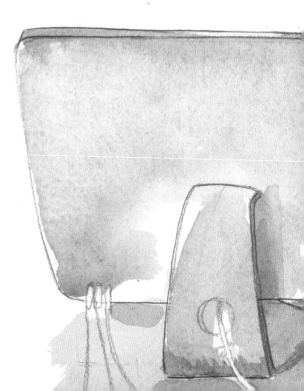

Every day for more than a week we worked on our reports, writing, researching, and rewriting. On the last day my teacher took out crayons and other art supplies and we drew portraits of the people in our reports.

We put the reports and drawings in the hallway so everyone in my school could see them. We had a party and my teacher took lots of pictures of us next to our projects.

My teacher loves to show everyone how much we know. Maybe that's why she keeps teaching.

If we finish all our work and we have time before the bell rings, my teacher tells us stories about the kids she once taught.

There is the story of city councilman Mr. Marino. "When Mr. Marino was in my class, he looked a mess. His shirt was always wrinkled and hanging outside his pants, and those pants often had holes in them. Who would have imagined he'd be working at City Hall?" asks my teacher.

PENGUIN

City Councilman
Chris Marino
Supports School

And then there are the stories about Annette Williams, who complained about being sick every day. "If she didn't have a headache, she had a tummy ache or a rash," my teacher says. "She spent more time in the nurse's office than in class."

When I visit her in her office, I call her "Dr. Williams."

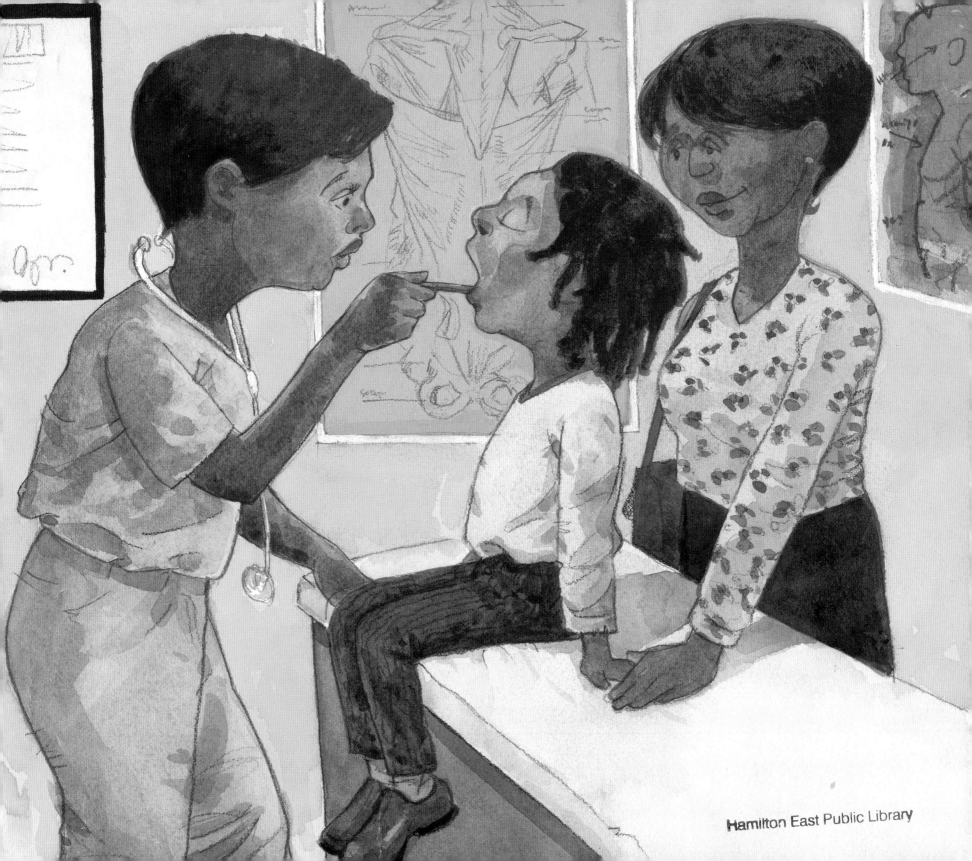

Hamilton East Public Library

Today she told us about a little girl who sat right in the corner over there and dreamed of being a teacher. I raised my hand and asked, "What happened to her?" My teacher smiled and pointed at herself and said, "I was that little girl."

Then I asked, "So is that why you keep teaching? Because it was your dream?"

My teacher replied, "I teach because of every one of *you*. I just love teaching and being a part of your lives. I love helping to make *your* dreams come true."

My teacher is the greatest. We are lucky that she is happy teaching right here at our school.